The American Dream Delayed:
The Harada Family's Quest for
Civil Rights

**Funded by a
Library Services & Technology Act (LSTA) grant**

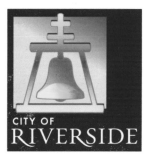

Riverside Public Library

Blue Jay In The Desert

Written By Marlene Shigekawa　　　　　*Illustrated By Isao Kikuchi*

Library of Congress Cataloging-in-Publication Data

Shigekawa, Marlene, 1944
Blue Jay In The Desert / by Marlene Shigekawa
illustrated by Isao Kikuchi

      p. cm.

Summary: While living in a relocation camp during the World
War II, a young Japanese American boy receives a message of
hope from his grandfather.

ISBN No. 1-879965-04-6: $12.95

1. Japanese Americans -- Evacuation and relocation,
1942-1945 - Juvenile Fiction. [1. Japanese
Americans -- Evacuation and relocation,
1942-1945 -- Fiction. 2. Grandfathers -- Fiction.]

I. Isao Kikuchi, ill. II. Title.

PZ7.S5554Bl   1993
[E] -- dc20   92-35424
                    CIP
                    AC

This is a New Book, Written and Illustrated
Especially for Polychrome Books
First Edition, May, 1993

Designed, produced and published by
Polychrome Publishing Corporation
4509 North Francisco Avenue, Chicago, Illinois
60625-3808
(312) 478-4455 Fax: (312) 478-0786

Printed in Hong Kong

10 9 8 7 6 5 4 3 2
ISBN 1-879965-04-6

For all the men in my family who helped pave the way
for our women to succeed:

Rinsaburo Ishii
Motojiro Shigekawa
Kiyoshi Shigekawa
Gerald Kiyoshi Shigekawa

And For Quincy who brings
her special gifts to the world.

--Marlene Shigekawa

To Junie and John

--Isao Kikuchi

Junior awoke in the darkness and heard the desert wind howling. It howled like the coyotes singing their nightly song, AH-OU-OU.

He heard his father muttering to himself. Junior called out, "Daddy, Daddy, what are you doing?"

"I'm trying to keep out the sand," Daddy whispered. His father was hanging a wet Army blanket in front of the door, as he always did when the dust storms blew angrily.

The fierce wind screeched louder. It rattled the door and begged to come inside. "Daddy, we're going to be blown over!"

In the dark, his father found him, gave him a hug and tucked him into bed. "Go back to sleep. Everything will be okay." Junior felt safer now.

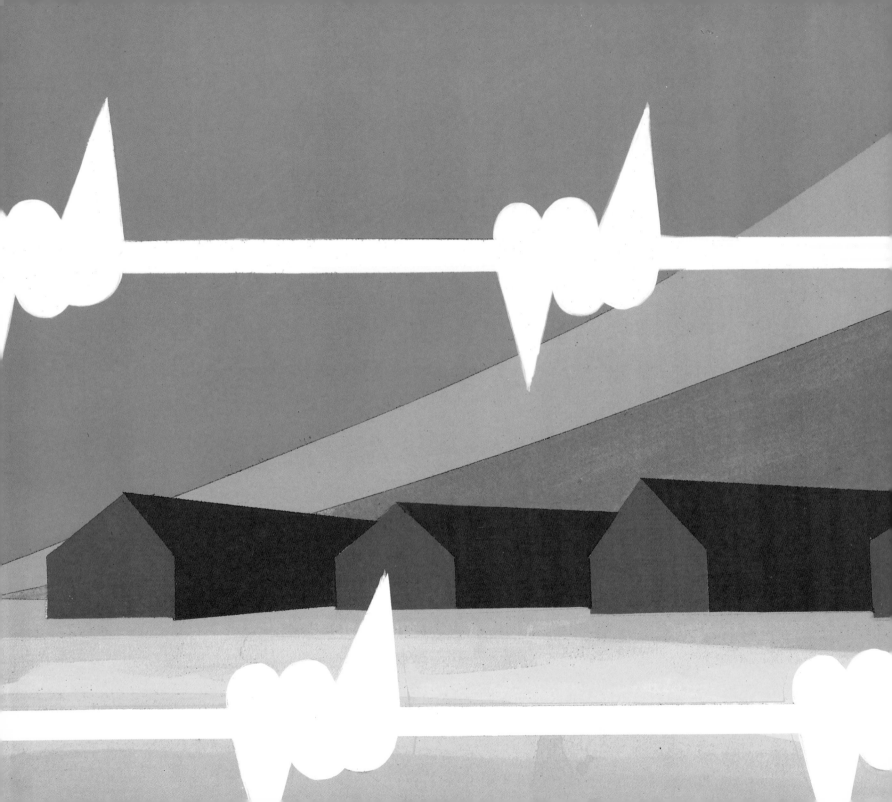

A long time ago Junior and his family lived far away in California. Now they lived in a camp in Poston, Arizona with thousands of other Japanese American families.
They were forced to leave their homes and belongings behind and move to this distant location. They called it an internment camp. Junior had been disappointed to find it wasn't anything like the camp he had imagined. There were no green forests, or tents, or singing around campfires. This camp had only dust and desert and more dust. Sometimes Junior would hear his mother and Grandpa sigh wistfully, and he would know they were missing their old home in California. Junior could hardly remember the cozy house they had left behind.

Morning came quickly. Junior
jumped out of bed and looked
outside for Grandpa.
He found him in his
usual place, sitting on
a wooden orange crate,
carving a piece of wood.
Grandpa was known
in the camp as a gifted
woodcarver.
Sometimes he carved horses,
their manes flying
as they raced faster than
the wind.
Sometimes he carved
delicate butterflies with colorful
wings that fluttered next to
flowers.
Grandpa's carvings were
something everyone wanted
to have.

A tattered straw hat protected
Grandpa's wrinkled face
and smiling eyes from
the harsh sun.
Back in California
his eyes looked as if they
were smiling all the time.
Only when sorrow covered
his face did his eyes lose
their twinkle.

Ever since they had come to Poston, Grandpa's eyes
hardly twinkled at all.But when he was carving, his eyes
twinkled as they had before.

Junior nestled next to him. He watched Grandpa's brown hands,
parched like the cracked earth, twist and turn the knife to free
the horse or butterfly or whatever animal was inside
the wood. Then, with his bright colored
paints, he would blow life into it.

"What are you making?" Junior asked.

Grandpa turned to Junior,
"This one is for you, Junior. What do you think?"
For him! Junior felt a big smile tickle his face. "For me!
What is it going to be?"

"Can't you tell?" teased Grandpa with a chuckle
as he held the block of wood up, down and sideways.

"A lion? A fish? Maybe a buffalo?" guessed Junior.
He hoped it would be a stallion or a great bear
or even a sea turtle swimming in the ocean.

Grandpa smiled and shook his head. "It's going to be a blue jay."

A blue jay?
Junior felt the smile leave his face.

A blue jay?
Just an itty bitty blue bird?
That wasn't exciting.
"Couldn't you make it an eagle...
or a crane?" he suggested.

Grandpa smiled again
and shook his head. "I think
that a blue jay will be just right,
and in time you will
come to like this blue jay."

Junior looked down at the hard,
dry ground.
Why would Grandpa make him
a tiny blue bird instead of
a ferocious beast?

Grandpa continued his carving.
"Someday when you know more about
blue jays and about the world, you'll
understand."

He paused for a moment.
"When I worked on the farm at home,
I liked to watch the blue jays.
I used to watch them
hunt and peck for food.
Sometimes I threw old dry bread
crumbs to them.
They came back to the same place day
after day. Blue jays are our friends."

The rhythm of Grandpa's hands made
Junior dreamy, and he tried to think
about what Grandpa had said.
Maybe Grandpa was right.
Maybe there was something more to
blue jays. He would try to find out.

There were not many books
in the internment camp.
Only a few made any mention of blue jays.
So, Junior asked everyone he knew to tell him
whatever they knew about blue jays.

"They fly quickly," said his mother,
"and the males have brighter blue feathers
than the females."

"They're not afraid to be angry,"
said his father.

"They eat insects and help the farmers,"
said Mr. Kumagai, the neighbor
in the next barrack.

"They live in the woods and fly across
the hills and valleys," said Mrs. Yoshimura
who worked in the mess hall.

"Their song goes like this,"
cawed Mrs. Logan, the school teacher.

Slowly, Junior collected more and more information about blue jays. Still, he didn't understand why Grandpa would choose to carve a blue jay for him. Sometimes, while he would watch Grandpa work, he would try to get Grandpa to tell him what the blue jay meant, but Grandpa would only say, "In time you will know."

Each day Grandpa and Junior walked along the barbed wire fence near the guard tower where the soldiers stood watch. Grandpa and Junior would look at the great desert surrounding them to see if anything had changed.
Each day was much like the day before.

But one day they were suddenly startled by the pounding of horse hooves. Junior tightly grasped Grandpa's sweaty hand. Two men on horseback stopped by the guarded gates before riding toward Grandpa and Junior. The men wore their shiny black hair in long braids, and their skin was tan from the hot desert sun.

"Who are they?" Junior asked.

"They're our neighbors. They're Mojave Indians," Grandpa explained. "They live on the Indian reservation. Their families have lived here for many, many years, even before Columbus came to America."

Junior's father appeared. One of the men handed him a woven red pouch.

"Here is some corn to plant to help feed your people. We know what it is like to be moved away from our homes."

"Thank you," his father said gratefully. Junior's father lowered his head slightly, showing respect in the Japanese way.

Junior thought it was nice of these men
to share their corn.
As the men rode away, Junior's father turned to
Grandpa and handed him the red pouch
filled with seeds.

"We can plant this in our victory garden."

"Why do we call it a victory garden?"
Junior asked. It seemed that he was always
asking questions these days.

"Because it is our way of helping during wartime
when fresh food is hard to get."

Junior helped plant the precious seeds
in their victory garden.

That night Junior thought more about the Mojaves who had given them the corn and who knew about trying to make a new home. As he fell asleep, he had a dream about his blue jay. It grew larger and larger until its wings could spread across the midnight sky. He climbed upon its wide back, and they soared into the sky. They flew over the barbed wire fence, beyond the guard tower where the soldiers stood watch, and high above the mountains to California. His blue jay took him home.

In the morning when Junior awoke,
he remembered his dream and what
Grandpa said about blue jays,
"They're our friends."

Then he thought, "This blue jay is like us.
We all want to go home where we belong.
This blue jay doesn't belong here either.
Blue jays belong in the woods . . . not
in the desert . . . a blue jay in the desert?"

Junior impatiently waited with his mother
in the line for breakfast in the mess hall.
He couldn't wait to tell Grandpa about his
dream. He found him after breakfast in his
usual place, sitting on his orange crate
and wearing his tattered straw hat.

"Grandpa!" shouted Junior running to him.
"Now I know about blue jays.
I can't wait for mine to be done."
Then he noticed that Grandpa was staring at
something in his cupped hands.

"Your blue jay is done. Here it is." Junior took
the shiny blue jay into his small hands.
His eyes were captivated by it for a long time.
He rubbed its smooth surface
and imagined that he felt its soft feathers.

"What a pretty little bird," said Mrs. Yoshimura who was passing by.

"It's more than that," replied Junior seriously. "It's my friend." Then he gave Grandpa a big grin. "It's like us and doesn't belong here."

Grandpa smiled and nodded, "Yes, blue jays are loyal and brave and always find a way to survive, like us."

Then he added, "Let this blue jay help you remember who you are and where you came from."

Junior gazed into his Grandpa's face,
swallowed hard and said nothing.
He understood.

Just then Junior's father came running up.
"Have you heard? Have you heard?"

Junior's mother came outside.
"What is it?" she asked worriedly.

Junior's father took a deep breath.
His voice became soft and gentle
as he announced, "We finally get to go home.
We'll be leaving soon."

Junior's mother cried with happiness, while Grandpa's smiling eyes sparkled like the desert stars.

Junior whispered to his blue jay, "No more blue jays in the desert. We're going home."

THE END

The Internment of Japanese Americans

Blue Jay In The Desert takes place during World War II. After President Franklin D. Roosevelt signed Executive Order 9066 on February 19, 1942, over 120,000 Japanese Americans were forced to leave their homes to be interned in relocation camps. These camps were located in barren, desolate areas of the country. The internees were imprisoned behind barbed wire and guard towers manned by armed soldiers. They were imprisoned but no charges were brought against them, no trials were held and no exceptions were granted. Poston, where this story is set, was one such place.

Attempts were made to justify the internment as necessary for the protection of the nation from espionage and sabotage. This was a poor excuse given the scope of the internment(which included infants and children as well as the elderly and infirm). In reality the internment was part of a long history of racism and prejudice against those of Asian ancestry that included Exclusion Acts and Alien Land Laws.

The last internment camp was closed in 1946 but it was not until the enactment of the Civil Liberties Act of 1988 that redress was achieved for those Japanese Americans who had been interned. On October 9,1990, the first redress check and government apology was presented. Sadly, many of those who suffered the internment did not live to see redress. In honor of their memory, it is incumbent upon us to combat racism and prejudice and protect the civil rights of ourselves and others.

Polychrome Publishing Corporation

Acknowledgments

Polychrome Publishing Corporation appreciates the encouragement and assistance rendered by Sam Ozaki, Harue Ozaki, Calvin Manshio, Peggy C. Wallace, Ashraf Manji, Philip Wong, Irene Cualoping, Carole Yoshida, Kiyo Yoshimura, William Yoshino, Anne Shimojima, Michael and Kay Janis, and Joyce MW Jenkin as well as the interest and enthusiastic support received from the Asian American community.

Marlene Shigekawa wishes to thank Lori Murakami, Cynthia Chin-Lee and Alan E.Young for their help.

For my parents and for you, Gerhard

Macmillan Publishing Company
866 Third Avenue, New York, N.Y. 10022
First American edition 1985
Printed in Great Britain
10 9 8 7 6 5 4 3 2 1
Library of Congress Cataloging in Publication Data
Kubler, Susanne.
    The three friends.
    Summary: Duffel the bear and Sam the long-eared
hare help their friend Cat become appreciated as a
storyteller instead of ridiculed as a liar.
    1. Children's stories, English. [1. Animals—Fiction.
2. Storytelling—Fiction] I. Title.
PZ7.K94845Th 1985   [E]   85-288
ISBN 0-02-751150-2 (Macmillan)

THE THREE FRIENDS

Written and illustrated by
Susanne Kubler

Macmillan Publishing Company
New York

Plop! The letter fell on the doormat at 4 Paw Corner
just as Duffel the bear and Sam the long-eared hare
were settling down for a Saturday afternoon snooze.
Duffel picked it up and read it to himself.
Then he read it out loud so there could be
no mistake about what it said:

> *Cat, the Adventurer,*
> *will be visiting his friends*
> *Duffel and Sam*
> *on Saturday afternoon*
> *at five o'clock.*

That was today!

Cat was a famous adventurer who traveled
all over the world. Once a year he came to see
his two friends in their cozy house at Paw Corner.

The two friends hurried to get everything ready
for their important visitor.
"I'll bake a cake," said Duffel, and he began to pour
great mounds of flour and honey into a bowl.
He always made double the quantity
so he could eat some while he was mixing.

Sam got the house ready. He tested all the cushions
for softness and dug up the best vegetables
from the garden.

At exactly five o'clock the great garden bell rang.
There, loaded down with bags, stood Cat.

"Close your eyes," he said as soon as he got inside.
"I've got a surprise for both of you."

The animals couldn't wait to see their presents.
"For Duffel," said Cat, "a sunshade that
turns into an umbrella when it's raining.
And for Sam, an earbrush that was given to me
by the King of Australia." Duffel and Sam had
never seen such wonderful presents in all their lives.

That night they sat up listening to Cat's amazing
adventures. He told them about the Eskimos
he had met in Africa, about flying hares who
lived at the top of trees and about a land
where honey lollipops grew like buttercups.

Duffel and Sam wished that they could have
adventures like Cat's.

When they could no longer keep their eyes open
the three animals went to bed. Sam dreamt
he could fly like the hares in Cat's story
and Duffel dreamt that he lived in
a land full of honey lollipops.

The next day the animals decided
to take Cat to their favorite picnic spot.
They filled the big basket with good things
to eat: raspberry puddings, chocolate cakes,
honey lollipops and carrots.

They took their large pink tablecloth
to sit on and, of course,
Duffel's new sunshade.

They set everything out by the river.
After they had all eaten more than they should
Cat asked, "Did I ever tell you how
I came across that rather special bag of mine?"
Duffel and Sam shook their heads.
"Well," he said, "Listen carefully."
And he sat back and began to tell them
the most fantastic tale of all.

"I was out walking by the river in a very hot land when I
found a bag hidden in the rushes. I knew at once
it belonged to the giant who lived in the mountains
for it was full of the treasure he had stolen from my friend
the King many years before."

"Anyway," Cat went on, "I had just picked it up when I felt
the earth tremble. The giant was coming. Suddenly his
great shadow blocked out the sun. As I ran with the bag
the lock snapped open and the treasure fell out. Of course,
the King never did get his gold back but he gave me
the bag to keep as a reward for my bravery."

Duffel and Sam had never heard such an exciting story.
Their friend was a true hero. They begged him to tell
more stories and they sat listening late into the afternoon.

When they finally set off, they met
Beaver, Badger and Raccoon standing
round a tree.

"Look who has come to stay," said Duffel proudly.
"Our friend Cat, the great adventurer."
"Huh! A fine friend *he* is," said Beaver,
pointing to a poster pinned to the tree.
It said:

WARNING!
THIS CAT
TELLS LIES

"That can't be true," said Duffel. But
when he turned round Cat had disappeared.

Duffel and Sam just could not believe it.
How could Cat have lied to them?
There was nothing left to do but go home.

"It's not the same without Cat," said Sam.
"Even though his stories were untrue,
I did enjoy hearing them."
"So did I," said Duffel.

Both animals felt so miserable
they decided to get their flashlight
and set off to look for Cat.

Duffel and Sam searched everywhere.
After what seemed a long time they came
very near the center of the forest.

"Shh!" said Duffel. "I think I can hear something."
The faint sound of sobbing came through the trees.

They pushed their way through the bushes and there,
looking tired, ragged and terribly unhappy, sat Cat.

"Oh, I wish you'd never found me," he said.
"I'm so ashamed that I told lies. It's just that
I do love telling stories."
Sam picked up Cat's bag and Duffel took Cat's paw,
and together the three friends set off home.

Before they went to bed the animals came up with a plan.
The next morning Duffel and Sam sent out an invitation
to all their friends. It read:

CAT
Professional Storyteller,
invites all the animals to hear his stories.
Stories invented on request.
No thinking time required.
All subjects covered –
Kings, giants, treasure, princesses,
looking glasses, et cetera, et cetera.

From that day onward Cat's fame spread far and wide,
and animals came from miles around to hear his tales.